RACE RELATIONS

Race Relations

A THOUGHT-PROVOKING COLLECTIBLE SHORT STORY

Walter the Educator

Silent King Books

SILENT KING BOOKS

SKB

Copyright © 2024 by Walter the Educator

All rights reserved. No part of this book may be reproduced in any manner whatsoever without written permission except in the case of brief quotations embodied in critical articles and reviews.

First Printing, 2024

Disclaimer
This book is a literary work; the story is not about specific persons, locations, situations, and/or circumstances unless mentioned in a historical context. Any resemblance to real persons, locations, situations, and/or circumstances is coincidental. This book is for entertainment and informational purposes only. The author and publisher offer this information without warranties expressed or implied. No matter the grounds, neither the author nor the publisher will be accountable for any losses, injuries, or other damages caused by the reader's use of this book. The use of this book acknowledges an understanding and acceptance of this disclaimer.

In Race Relations, a White man tries to befriend a black woman to receive a BIG tax credit from the government.

In a time not far from our own, in a country frayed by deep-seated racial discord, the government sought to heal its fractured society through a novel initiative. Desperation birthed the "Unity Credit," a bold policy offering a $25,000 tax credit to any citizen who could prove a genuine friendship with someone of a different race. It was a radical plan, met with skepticism and hope in equal measure.

Race Relations

Ethan Matthews, a white man in his early thirties, was struggling to make ends meet. His job at a small marketing firm barely covered his bills, and the idea of an extra $25,000 was more than appealing—it was life changing. However, the stipulations of the Unity Credit were strict: proof of a deep, authentic bond was required. Ethan pondered his options and decided to befriend someone outside his racial comfort zone.

Race Relations

He had seen her before, the woman who always seemed to be in a hurry, her presence commanding and her demeanor resolute. Her name was Aaliyah Brown, a black woman working in the same office building as Ethan. She was a software engineer, known for her brilliance and no-nonsense attitude. Ethan decided she would be his key to the coveted tax credit.

Race Relations

Their first encounter was awkward, to say the least. Ethan approached Aaliyah in the elevator one morning, attempting small talk about the weather. She responded politely but curtly, her guard clearly up. Undeterred, Ethan continued his efforts, striking up conversations whenever their paths crossed. He asked about her work, her interests, and even shared anecdotes from his life. Each interaction was met with the same polite distance.

Race Relations

One rainy afternoon, Ethan mustered the courage to ask Aaliyah out for coffee. She hesitated, her eyes narrowing as if trying to see through his intentions. "Why?" she asked bluntly. Ethan, caught off guard, stammered, "I just thought it would be nice to get to know each other better." Aaliyah's lips tightened into a thin line. "Is this about the Unity Credit?" she asked, her voice sharp and accusatory. Ethan's face flushed. "No, it's not like that," he lied. "I just think you're interesting and would like to be friends."

Race Relations

Aaliyah studied him for a moment, then shook her head. "I'm sorry, but I don't have time for forced friendships." With that, she walked away, leaving Ethan standing in the lobby, feeling both exposed and defeated. The next few weeks were a series of similar rejections. Aaliyah's responses ranged from polite dismissals to outright refusals. She seemed to see through every attempt Ethan made, perceiving them as insincere. The more he tried, the more transparent his motives became.

Race Relations

Frustration and desperation began to cloud Ethan's judgment. He needed that money, but every attempt to connect with Aaliyah felt contrived and artificial. He spent hours researching her interests, hoping to find common ground, but each interaction only solidified her perception of him as disingenuous.

Race Relations

One evening, as he sat in his cramped apartment, surrounded by bills and a dwindling bank balance, Ethan had an epiphany. His approach had been all wrong. He had been so focused on the end goal—the tax credit—that he had forgotten the essence of what he was supposed to be achieving, a genuine friendship. He realized that to earn Aaliyah's trust, he had to be authentic. He needed to see her not as a means to an end, but as a person with her own experiences and emotions.

Race Relations

The next day, Ethan decided to take a different approach. He waited for Aaliyah in the lobby after work, not with a rehearsed speech or a hidden agenda, but with a simple, honest intention. When she appeared, he walked up to her, his heart pounding." Aaliyah, can I talk to you for a minute?" he asked. She sighed, clearly weary of his persistence. "Ethan, if this is another attempt—"

Race Relations

"It's not," he interrupted. "I just want to apologize. I've been going about this all wrong. I was so focused on the tax credit that I forgot what it means to be a friend. I'm sorry if I made you feel like a project or a target. That was never my intention." Aaliyah looked at him, her expression unreadable. "So, what do you want now?" "I want to start over," Ethan said sincerely. "No agendas, no ulterior motives. Just two people trying to get to know each other." Aaliyah studied him for a long moment, then nodded slowly. "Alright. Let's see where this goes."

Race Relations

The days that followed marked a significant shift in their interactions. Ethan no longer approached Aaliyah with rehearsed lines or forced conversations. Instead, he listened. He learned about her passion for coding, her love for jazz music, and her struggles as a black woman in a predominantly white industry. In turn, he shared his own challenges, his dreams, and his fears.

Race Relations

Their conversations became more natural, more fluid. They discovered common interests and debated their differences. Ethan began to see Aaliyah not as a ticket to financial relief but as a person with her own unique perspectives and experiences. He respected her resilience, admired her intelligence, and found himself genuinely enjoying her company.

Race Relations

One evening, over coffee, Aaliyah shared a story from her childhood. She spoke of growing up in a racially charged neighborhood, the prejudice she faced, and the strength it took to overcome it. Ethan listened intently, moved by her courage and resilience. "You know," Aaliyah said, stirring her coffee thoughtfully, "when you first approached me, I thought you were just another person looking for a quick fix. But you've surprised me, Ethan. You've shown me that you're willing to learn and grow. That means a lot."

Ethan smiled, feeling a warmth in his chest that had nothing to do with the tax credit. "I'm glad to hear that. And I promise, no more agendas. Just friendship." Over time, their bond deepened. They attended jazz concerts together, explored new restaurants, and even took up a coding project as a team. Their friendship blossomed into something real, built on mutual respect and understanding.

Race Relations

When the time came to apply for the Unity Credit, both Ethan and Aaliyah had nearly forgotten about it. They had become true friends, their connection transcending the financial incentive that had initially brought them together. They submitted their application, providing evidence of their genuine friendship through photos, messages, and testimonials from colleagues who had witnessed their evolving bond. The government panel reviewed their case, and within weeks, both Ethan and Aaliyah received confirmation of their $25,000 tax credit.

Race Relations

But the money, once so desperately sought after, now felt secondary. For Ethan, the real reward was the friendship he had gained. He had not only earned a financial boost but had also grown as a person, learning to appreciate and value someone different from himself. Aaliyah, too, found value in their friendship. She had been wary of Ethan's intentions at first, but his persistence and eventual sincerity had proven that people could change, that genuine connections could be forged even in the most unlikely circumstances.

Race Relations

The Unity Credit program, while controversial and flawed, had achieved something remarkable in this instance. It had brought two people together, breaking down barriers and fostering understanding where there had once been mistrust.

Race Relations

Ethan and Aaliyah continued their friendship long after the tax credit had been spent. They supported each other through life's ups and downs, celebrating successes and comforting each other in times of need. Their story became a testament to the power of genuine human connection, transcending race and financial incentives.

Race Relations

In a country still grappling with racial tensions, their friendship stood as a beacon of hope. It showed that, despite the challenges and prejudices that existed, true understanding and unity were possible. The journey had been difficult, filled with trials and tribulations, but in the end, it had been worth every moment.

Race Relations

Through their bond, Ethan and Aaliyah demonstrated that the path to healing and unity lay not in grand gestures or financial incentives, but in the simple, everyday acts of kindness, respect, and genuine friendship. Their story became a reminder that, even in the most turbulent of times, the human spirit could rise above division and find common ground.

Race Relations

And so, in a nation struggling to mend its racial wounds, the friendship between a white man and a black woman became a symbol of what could be achieved when people opened their hearts and minds to one another. It was a story of transformation, of growth, and of the enduring power of true friendship.

Race Relations

As time passed, the story of Ethan and Aaliyah's friendship spread beyond their workplace and social circles. It became a symbol of hope and resilience in a nation still wrestling with the ghosts of its past. The media caught wind of their journey, and soon they were being interviewed on local news channels, podcasts, and even invited to speak at community events.

Race Relations

Their message was clear and consistent: true change starts with genuine human connections. They recounted their initial struggles, the awkward attempts at conversation, and the slow, steady development of mutual trust. Their story resonated with many, inspiring others to look beyond superficial differences and seek out real, meaningful relationships.

Race Relations

The impact of their friendship extended beyond the two of them. In their office building, a once-polarized environment began to shift. Colleagues of different races started interacting more openly, encouraged by Ethan and Aaliyah's example. The cafeteria, once divided along racial lines, now buzzed with mixed groups engaging in lively discussions. The office formed a diversity committee, and initiatives aimed at fostering inclusivity and understanding were implemented.

Race Relations

Meanwhile, Ethan's and Aaliyah's personal lives flourished. Ethan, who had always been somewhat reserved, found himself more open and empathetic, qualities that improved not just his friendships but his professional relationships as well. He received a promotion, not just because of his work ethic, but because he had become a more effective and compassionate leader.

Race Relations

Aaliyah, on the other hand, became a mentor to young women of color entering the tech field. She used her platform to advocate for diversity in the industry, drawing from her own experiences to inspire and guide others. Her friendship with Ethan served as a cornerstone of her message: that true allyship requires effort, understanding, and a willingness to learn and grow together.

Race Relations

Their bond deepened further when they decided to embark on a joint project aimed at bridging racial divides through technology. Combining Ethan's marketing expertise and Aaliyah's coding skills, they developed an app called "Unity Connect." The app matched people from different racial and cultural backgrounds, encouraging them to meet, share experiences, and build friendships. It featured guided activities, conversation starters, and resources on cultural competence.

Race Relations

Unity Connect quickly gained traction, supported by organizations and communities eager to foster better race relations. Schools adopted the app as part of their diversity and inclusion programs, while companies used it to improve workplace culture. The app's success underscored the idea that technology, when used thoughtfully, could be a powerful tool for social change.

Race Relations

As their lives intertwined further, Ethan and Aaliyah's friendship faced new challenges. They encountered backlash from those who saw their efforts as forced or insincere. Some accused them of exploiting their story for personal gain. These criticisms tested their resolve, but they stood firm, knowing that their bond was genuine and their mission important.

Race Relations

One particularly harsh critique came from a well-known commentator who dismissed the Unity Credit program as a "shallow gimmick" and labeled Ethan and Aaliyah's friendship as a "convenient narrative." Hurt but undeterred, they decided to confront the criticism head-on by writing an open letter, published in a major newspaper.

Race Relations

In the letter, they candidly addressed their initial motivations, acknowledging the flaws and insecurities they had faced. They detailed the evolution of their relationship, emphasizing the authenticity that had emerged from their shared experiences and mutual respect. They ended the letter with a call to action, urging others to look beyond cynicism and take the first steps towards understanding and friendship.

Race Relations

The letter went viral, sparking conversations across the nation. People from all walks of life shared their own stories of cross-racial friendships, creating a groundswell of support for the idea that change, though difficult, was possible through personal connections.

Race Relations

The government, encouraged by the success stories and increased dialogue, expanded the Unity Credit program, introducing new measures to ensure its integrity and effectiveness. They implemented educational workshops on cultural competence and implicit bias, making these resources accessible to all citizens. The goal was to foster a deeper understanding and lasting relationships, rather than just incentivize superficial interactions.

Race Relations

Ethan and Aaliyah continued to be at the forefront of these initiatives. They traveled across the country, speaking at schools, community centers, and corporate events. Their message was always the same: real change requires real effort. They encouraged people to step out of their comfort zones, to listen and learn from each other, and to build bridges where there were once walls.

Race Relations

Their journey took an unexpected turn when they were invited to the White House to meet with the President. The administration wanted to recognize their contributions and discuss ways to further promote racial unity in the country. Standing in the Oval Office, Ethan and Aaliyah felt a sense of pride and responsibility. Their friendship, once a private struggle, had become a catalyst for national change.

Race Relations

During the meeting, they proposed a nationwide mentorship program that paired individuals from different racial backgrounds. The program, modeled after their own experiences, would focus on building genuine connections through shared activities and open dialogue. The President, impressed by their vision and dedication, pledged to support the initiative.

Race Relations

As the years went by, the mentorship program flourished, creating thousands of new friendships across the country. Ethan and Aaliyah watched with pride as people of all ages and backgrounds embraced the challenge of understanding and connecting with one another. The nation, still imperfect and grappling with its past, took significant steps towards healing and unity.

Race Relations

Ethan and Aaliyah's friendship remained a cornerstone of their lives. They celebrated milestones together, supported each other through personal struggles, and continued to learn from each other. Their bond was a testament to the power of persistence, empathy, and genuine human connection.

Race Relations

In a country once divided by racial strife, their story stood as a beacon of hope. It reminded people that, despite the obstacles and prejudices that existed, true understanding and friendship were possible. Ethan and Aaliyah's journey, filled with trials and triumphs, showed that the path to healing and unity lay not in grand gestures or superficial incentives, but in the simple, everyday acts of kindness, respect, and genuine human connection.

Race Relations

As they looked towards the future, they knew their work was far from over. But they also knew that, together, they had made a difference. And in a world often defined by its divisions, their friendship was a powerful reminder of what could be achieved when people opened their hearts and minds to one another.

Race Relations

ABOUT THE CREATOR

Walter the Educator is one of the pseudonyms for Walter Anderson. Formally educated in Chemistry, Business, and Education, he is an educator, an author, a diverse entrepreneur, and he is the son of a disabled war veteran. "Walter the Educator" shares his time between educating and creating. He holds interests and owns several creative projects that entertain, enlighten, enhance, and educate, hoping to inspire and motivate you.

Follow, find new works, and stay up to date
with Walter the Educator™
at WaltertheEducator.com

www.ingramcontent.com/pod-product-compliance
Lightning Source LLC
LaVergne TN
LVHW051926060526
838201LV00062B/4701